JN102690

TANKA
from FOREIGN TRAVELS
112 Tanka by Kazuo Kanai
in three languages

訳 —— 冨野光太郎
Translator / Traducteur —— Kotaro Tomino

監修 —— マクシアンヌ・バーガー
Editing and Research / Révision et Recherche —— Maxianne Berger

英仏訳

海外詠112首
金井一夫

TANKA
de VOYAGES à l'ÉTRANGER
112 tanka par Kazuo Kanai
en trois langues

深夜叢書社
Shinyasōsho-sha

目次

Table of Contents
Table des Matières

はじめに ──────────────────────────────────── 7

第1章 ──────────────────────────────────── 11

　英国：エディンバラ／ロンドン
　フィリピン：マニラ／コレヒドール
　米国：マンハッタン

第2章 ──────────────────────────────────── 29

　豪州：シドニー、韓国：ソウル
　中国：香港／九寨溝

第3章 ──────────────────────────────────── 37

　中国：上海、インド：ムンバイ
　ボツワナ、中国：成都

第4章 ──────────────────────────────────── 49

　ペルー：マチュピチュ、中国：北京
　チェコ：プラハ、中国：成都／敦煌

第5章 ──────────────────────────────────── 65

　マレーシア：クアラルンプール、ブラジル：アマゾン
　カンボジア：アンコール・ワット、中国：桂林
　ロシア：モスクワ／イルクーツク／バイカル湖

第6章 ──────────────── 83

ネパール：カトマンズ、台湾：台北

第7章 ──────────────── 91

米国：シアトル、フィリピン：マニラ
ボスニア・ヘルツェゴヴィナ：サラエボ
韓国：釜山、カンボジア：プノンペン

第8章 ──────────────── 105

ベトナム
ドイツ：ベルリン、モンゴル
バチカン市国：サン・ピエトロ

第9章 ──────────────── 121

ブータン、インド

第10章 ──────────────── 129

ロシア：サハリン、スリランカ
米国：ラスベガス／グランドキャニオン

訳者あとがき ──────────────── 139

プロフィール ──────────────── 143

Author's Preface ——————————————————————— 7

Chapter 1 ———————————————————————————— 11
Edinburgh, London/Great Britain
Manila, Corregidor/Philippines
Manhattan/USA

Chapter 2 ———————————————————————————— 29
Sydney/Australia, Seoul/The Republic of Korea
Hong Kong, Jiuzhaigou/China

Chapter 3 ———————————————————————————— 37
Shanghai/China, Munbai/India, Botswana, Chengdu/China

Chapter 4 ———————————————————————————— 49
Machu Picchu,/Peru, Beijing/China, Prague/Czechia
Chengdu, Dunhuang/Chin

Chapter 5 ———————————————————————————— 65
Kuala Lumpur/Malasia, Amazon/Brasil
Angkor Wat/Cambodia, Guilin/China
Moscow, Irkutsk, lake Baikal/Russia

Chapter 6 ———————————————————————————— 83
Katmandu/Nepal, Taipei/Taiwan

Chapter 7 ———————————————————————————— 91
Seattle/USA, Manila/Philipppines, Sarajevo/Bosnia & Herzegovina
Pusan/the Republic of Korea, Phnum Pénh/Cambodia

Chapter 8 ——————————————————————————— 105
Vietnam, Berlin/Germany, Mongolia, Saint Peter's Basilica/Vatican

Chapter 9 ——————————————————————————— 121
Bhutan, India

Chapter 10 —————————————————————————— 129
Sakhalin/Russia, Sri Lanka
Las Vegas, Grand Canyon/USA

Translator's Postface ———————————————————— 139
Profiles ——————————————————————————————— 143

Préface du poète ——————————————————— 7

Chapitre 1 ——————————————————————— 11
Édimbourg, Londres/Grande-Bretagne
Manille, Corregidor/Philippines
Manhattan/les États-Unis

Chapitre 2 ——————————————————————— 29
Sydney/Australie, Séoul/République de Corée,
Hong Kong, Jiuzhaigou/Chine

Chapitre 3 ——————————————————————— 37
Shanghai/Chine, Mumbai/Inde, Botswana, Chengdu/Chine

Chapitre 4 ——————————————————————— 49
Machu Picchu/Pérou, Pékin/Chine, Prague/La Tchéquie

Chapitre 5 ——————————————————————— 65
Kuala Lumpur/Malaisie, Amazonie/Brésil
Angkor Wat/Cambodge, Guilin/Chine
Moscou, Irkoutsk, Vladivostok, le lac Baïkal /Russie

Chapitre 6 ——————————————————————— 83
Katmandou/Népal, Taipei/Taïwan

Chapitre 7 ——————————————————————— 91
Seattle/les États-Unis, Manille/Philipppines, Sarajevo/Bosnie-Herzégovine
Pusan/République de Corée, Phnum Penh/Cambodgee

Chapitre 8 ——————————————————————— 105
Viêt Nam, Berlin/Allemagne, Mongolie, Basilique Saint-Pierre/Vatican

Chapitre 9 ——————————————————————— 121
Bhoutan, Inde

Chapitre 10 —————————————————————— 129
Sakhaline/Russie, Sri Lanka
Las Vegas, Grand Canyon/les États-Unis

Postface du Traducteur ——————————————— 139
Profils ————————————————————————— 143

はじめに

　2019年7月に出版した私の第一歌集『海外詠』(青磁社刊、557首所収)は、2000年から2018年の間、即ち、私が64歳から82歳までの時期に訪問した諸外国にて詠んだ短歌を集めた歌集です。その中から112首を選び、国際タンカ協会の冨野光太郎氏に英語と仏語の翻訳をお願いして本歌集が出来上がりました。

　私は小さい頃から読書に親しんできましたが、豊かな家庭ではありませんでした。父は薄給の警察官で留守がちであり、母はリュウマチで病弱、そして、3人の妹がいたため、中学2年から珠算塾の助手をしながら家計を助けていました。商業高校に入学して間もなく肺結核を患い、休学を繰り返し最終的に大学を卒業したのは25歳でした。その後、会計事務所に勤務し、30歳の時、公認会計士資格を得て現在も会計事務所を運営しています。

　従って、海外旅行は、若い時に始めたのではなく、先妻が病没した折、中学2年の娘を慰めるためハワイとカリフォルニアのディズニー・ランドへ行ったのが最初です。その後、仕事の関係で海外旅行の機会が飛躍的に増えました。直近では、2022年6月、カナダのモントリオールで開催された第104回国際ライオンズクラブの大会に参加しました。

　世界平和を祈念しつつ、この翻訳歌集が、世界各国の新しい読者の皆様に、共感を以って受け入れられることを願っています。

2023年3月1日

金井　一夫

Preface

My first tanka collection, *Kaigai-ei* (TANKA from FOREIGN TRAVELS), was published in Japanese in July, 2019, by the press Seijisha in Tokyo. It consists of 557 tanka written from 2000 to 2018, in foreign countries only, when I was 64 to 82 years old. I selected 112 of these and asked Kotaro Tomino, a member of the International Tanka Society in Tokyo, to translate them into English and French.

I have enjoyed reading since I was little, but my family was not rich. My father was a poorly-paid policeman who was often away from home. My mother suffered from rheumatism, and I had three younger sisters. In my second year of junior high school, I started helping with housework while working as a teaching assistant at an abacus school. Shortly after entering a commercial high school, I was stricken with pulmonary tuberculosis and had to miss school several times for long periods. So, it was at the age of 25 that I finally graduated from university in Tokyo. After that, I started working in an accounting firm and at the age of 30 I obtained the diploma of Chartered Public Accountant. Today, I still run the accounting firm that I founded.

Therefore, I didn't start travelling abroad when I was young. When my first wife passed away from an illness, to comfort my daughter who was in her second year of junior high school, we visited Hawaii and Disneyland in California. It was my first trip abroad. Since then, owing to work, my opportunities to travel abroad have increased considerably. Most recently, in June 2022, I attended the 104th Lions Clubs International Convention in Montreal, Canada.

Finally, as I pray for world peace, I hope this collection of translated tanka will be accepted with empathy by many new readers in various countries.

March 1, 2023
Kazuo Kanai

Préface

Mon premier recueil de tanka, *Kaigai-ei* (TANKA de VOYAGES à l'ÉTRANGER), a été publié en japonais en juillet 2019 à Tokyo par la maison d'édition Seijisha, et contient 557 tanka. Cela couvre la période entre 2000 et 2018, c'est-à-dire, quand j'avais de 64 à 82 ans. Tous les tanka ont été écrits uniquement dans des pays étrangers. J'en ai sélectionné 112 et j'ai demandé à Kotaro Tomino, membre de l'International Tanka Society à Tokyo, de les traduire en anglais et en français.

Depuis que j'étais petit, j'aimais lire mais ma famille n'était pas riche. Mon père était un policier mal payé qui était souvent absent de chez nous. Ma mère souffrait de rhumatismes et j'avais trois sœurs plus jeunes. En deuxième année de secondaire, j'ai commencé à aider avec le ménage tout en travaillant comme assistant d'enseignement dans une école de boulier. Peu de temps après être entré dans un lycée commercial, j'ai été atteint de tuberculose pulmonaire et j'ai dû manquer longtemps plusieurs fois l'école. Du coup, c'est à l'âge de 25 ans que j'ai finalement obtenu mon diplôme d'université à Tokyo. Après cela, j'ai commencé à travailler dans un cabinet de service comptable et j'ai obtenu à l'âge de 30 ans le diplôme d'expert-comptable. Maintenant, je dirige toujours le cabinet comptable que j'ai créé.

Donc, je n'ai pas commencé à voyager à l'étranger quand j'étais jeune. Lorsque ma première femme est décédée des suites d'une maladie, afin de réconforter ma fille qui était en deuxième année de secondaire, nous avons visité Hawaï et Disneyland en Californie. C'était mon premier voyage à l'étranger. Depuis lors, grâce à mon travail, mes opportunités de voyager à l'étranger ont considérablement augmenté. Plus récemment, en juin 2022, j'ai assisté à la 104ème convention du Lions Clubs Internationaux à Montréal, au Canada.

Finalement, en priant pour la paix mondiale, je souhaite que ce recueil de tanka traduits soit accepté avec empathie par de nombreux nouveaux lecteurs dans les divers pays.

le premier mars 2023
Kazuo Kanai

第1章
Chapter 1 (2000-2001)

page 12-20 ——— 英国：エディンバラ、ロンドン
Edinburgh, London, Great Britain
Édimbourg, Londres, Grande-Bretagne

page 21-25 ——— フィリピン：コレヒドール
Manila, Corregidor, Philippines
Manille, Corregidor, Philippines

page 26-27 ——— 米国：マンハッタン
Manhattan, USA
Manhattan, les États-Unis

牧草の照りしづかなる丘陵は
青なる天に抱かれてをり

the quiet hill
covered with
shining pasture
is embraced
by the blue sky

la colline tranquille
recouverte de
pâturage brillant
est accueillie
par le ciel bleu

ぼくそうのてりしずかなるきゅうりょうは
bokusō no teri shizuka naru kyūryō wa

あおなるてんにいだかれており
ao naru ten ni idakare te ori

夕空に輪郭浮かぶ牛の群れ
丘の暮色に首みな垂れて

cows
are silhouetted against
the evening sky
all heads bowing
on the hill at dusk

des vaches
se révèlent en silhouette
contre le ciel du soir
toute tête baissée
sur la colline au crépuscule

ゆうぞらにりんかくうかぶうしのむれ
yūzora ni rinkaku ukabu ushi no mure

おかのぼしょくにくびみなたれて
oka no boshoku ni kubi mina tare te

中世のエディンバラ城が町抱かへ
夕日浴びつつ緋色に迫る

Edinburgh Castle
built in the Middle Ages
appears to be scarlet
embracing the town and
basking in the setting sun

le château d'Édimbourg
construit au moyen âge
paraît écarlate
embrassant la ville et
se dorant au soleil couchant

ちゅうせいのエディンバラじょうがまちかかえ
chūsei no edinbara jō ga machi kakae

ゆうひあびつつひいろにせまる
yūhi abi tsutsu hiiro ni semaru

亡き妻をしばし想へりウインダミア
湖水の上の白き浮雲

a white floating cloud
reflected in lake Windermere
reminds me
for a moment
of my late wife

un nuage blanc flottant
son reflet dans le lac Windermere
me fait penser
un moment
à ma défunte femme

なきつまをしばしおもえりウィンダミア
naki tsuma wo shibashi omoe ri windamia

こすいのうえのしろきうきぐも
kosui no ue no shiroki ukigumo

トルコ石で装飾されたる頭骸骨
眼窩も大英博物館のもの

the exhibit of
an ancient skull decorated
with turquoise stones
even both eye sockets
belong to the British Museum

l'exposition
d'un ancien crâne décoré
en pierres de turquoise
même ses deux orbites
appartiennent au British Museum

トルコいしでそうしょくされたるずがいこつ
torukoishi de sōshoku sare taru zugaikotsu

がんかもだいえいはくぶつかんのもの
ganka mo daiei hakubutsukan no mono

遥かなる身内の悲しみ聞かむかに
ミイラは手合わせ横向きに眠る

hands crossed in prayer
a mummy sleeps
on its side
as if sharing the grief
of distant relatives

les mains croisées en prière
une momie dort
sur le côté
comme si elle partageait
le chagrin de parents éloignés

はるかなるみうちのかなしみきかんかに
haruka naru miuchi no kanashimi kikan ka ni

ミイラはてあわせよこむきにねむる
mīra wa te awase yokomuki ni nemuru

テムズ河の濁れる水が石を打ち
石段のぼれば断頭台なり

muddy water
from the Thames
laps against riverside stones
I go up the stone steps
that lead me to a guillotine

l'eau boueuse de la Tamise
clapote sur les pierres
de la rive
je monte les marches en pierre
qui me mènent à la guillotine

テムズがわのにごれるみずがいしをうち
temuzu gawa no nigoreru mizu ga ishi wo uchi

いしだんのぼればだんとうだいなり
ishidan nobore ba dantōdai nari

ダイアナ妃も妻もこの世に今は亡く
ケンジントン宮殿夕風寒し

neither Princess Diana
nor my wife is alive
in this world
I visit Kensington Palace
the evening's cold breeze

ni la princesse Diana
ni ma femme
ne sont de ce monde
je visite le palais de Kensington
la brise froide du soir

ダイアナひもつまもこのよにいまはなく
daiana hi mo tsuma mo konoyo ni ima wa naku

ケンジントンきゅうでんゆうかぜさむし
kenjinton kyūden yūkaze samushi

薔薇色の空が紺へと暮れてゆく
旅の終わりのロンドンの街

the rose-coloured sky
is gradually darkening
into a navy blue
my trip is about
to end in London

le ciel rose
s'assombrit progressivement
en bleu marine
mon voyage est sur le point
de se terminer à Londre

ばらいろのそらがこんへとくれてゆく
barairo no sora ga kon e to kure te yuku

たびのおわりのロンドンのまち
tabi no owari no rondon no machi

水牛に妻乗せ夕日浴びながら
畔行く人を目にて追ひけり

I watch
the farmer follow
a causeway
bathed in evening sun
with his wife on a buffalo

je regarde
un agriculteur suivre
la chaussée
baigné du soleil du soir
avec sa femme sur un buffle

すいぎゅうにつまのせゆうひあびながら
suigyū ni tsuma nose yūhi abi nagara

あぜゆくひとをめにておいけり
aze yuku hito wo me nite oi keri

観光の目玉六千の日本兵の
自爆死跡地コルヒドールは

the suicide bombing
by six thousand Japanese soldiers
at Corregidor
it's a principal spot
for tourism

l'attentat-suicide à la bombe
de six mille soldats japonais
à Corregidor
c'est un centre majeur
de tourisme

かんこうのめだまろくせんのにほんへいの
kankō no medama roku sen no nihonhei no

じばくしあとちコレヒドールは
jibaku shi atochi koruhidōru wa

白骨の下に遺りしてふ五銭玉
赤銅色に変はりてありし

they say
a five-sen coin remained
under a soldier's skeleton
its colour has changed
to coppery red

on dit qu'il restait
une pièce de cinq sen
sous un squelette de soldat
sa couleur avait viré
au rouge cuivré

はっこつのしたにのこりしちょうごせんだま
hakkotsu no shita ni nokori shi chou gosendama

しゃくどういろにかわりてありし
shakudō iro ni kawari te ari shi

生還を願ひし母の五銭玉
兵士は握りし死にたるのちも

even after death
in his hand a soldier held
the five-sen coin*
his mother had given him
wishing for his safe return

*an old copper Japanese coin, symbol of escape from death

même après sa mort
un soldat tenait dans sa main
une pièce de cinq-sen*
sa mère le lui avait donné
désirant son retour sans encombre

*une ancienne monnaie de cuivre japonaise, symbole pour échapper à la mort.

せいかんをねがいしははのごせんだま
seikan wo negai shi haha no gosendama

へいしはにぎりししにたるのちも
heishi wa nigiri shi shini taru nochi mo

祖国向き眠る兵士に寄りそひて
慈悲観音が海際に立つ

facing towards the homeland
dead soldiers sleep in the cemetery
the Goddess of Mercy
stands alongside
on the seashore

dans la direction de la patrie
les soldats morts dorment au cimetière
la déesse de la miséricorde
se tient à côté
au bord de la mer

そこくむきねむるへいしによりそいて
sokoku muki nemuru heishi ni yorisoi te

じひかんのんがうみぎわにたつ
jihi kan'non ga umigiwa ni tatsu

ハドソン川の堤に寝ころび摩天楼
仰げるわれは常の旅人

lying back on
the bank of the Hudson River
I look up at
the skyscrapers
I'm always a traveler

m'allongeant sur
la berge du Hudson
je regarde
les gratte-ciel
je suis toujours un voyageur

ハドソンがわのつつみにねころびまてんろう
hadoson gawa no tsutsumi ni nekorobi matenrō

あおげるわれはつねのたびびと
aogeru ware wa tsune no tabibito

地下鉄の天井に触れわれに触れ
肩車の子の小さき指先

a toddler
being carried on shoulders
touches
the subway ceiling and my body
with his little fingertips

un bambin
porté sur des épaules
touche
du bout de ses petits doigts
le plafond du métro et mon corps

ちかてつのてんじょうにふれわれにふれ
chikatetsu no tenjō ni hure ware ni hure

かたぐるまのこのちさきゆびさき
kataguruma no ko no chīsaki yubisaki

第2章
Chapter 2 (2002-2004)

page 30 ──────── 豪州：シドニー
Sydney, Australia
Sydney, Australie

page 31 ──────── 韓国：ソウル
Seoul, The Republic of Korea
Séoul, République de Corée

page 32-33 ──────── 中国：香港
Hong Kong, China
Hong Kong, Chine

page 34-35 ──────── 中国：九寨溝
Jiuzhaigou, China
Jiuzhaigou, Chine

潮の香の淡き渚に佇めば
オペラハウスは夕日に輝く

on the shore
a faint scent of tide
I stand for a while
the Opera House shines
in the setting sun

sur le rivage
un parfum léger de marée
je reste un certain temps
le théâtre de l'Opéra brille
au soleil couchant

しおのかのあわきなぎさにたたずめば
shio no ka no awaki nagisa ni tatazume ba

オペラハウスはゆうひにかがやく
opera hausu wa yūhi ni kagayaku

決めつけて物言ふ人に諾はず
応ぜず仁川空港を発つ

neither agreeing with
nor answering
the person
who speaks arrogantly
I leave Incheon Airport

sans être d'accord
et sans répondre
à la personne
qui parle avec arrogance
je part de l'aéroport d'Incheon

きめつけてものいうひとにうべなわず
kimetsuke te mono iu hito ni ubenawa zu

おうぜずインチョンくうこうをたつ
ōze zu inchon kūkō wo tatsu

異国語の会議に疲れ窓みれば
カジノの船が夕日浴びゐる

feeling exhausted
after the conference in a foreign language
I look through the window
a casino-boat bathes
in the setting sun

me sentant épuisé
après la conférence en langue étrangère
je regarde par la fenêtre
un bateau-casino se baigne
au soleil couchant

いこくごのかいぎにつかれまどみれば
ikokugo no kaigi ni tsukare mado mire ba

カジノのふねがゆうひあびゐる
kajino no fune ga yūhi abi iru

海近き苑にひととき真似をれば
太極拳の息ながかりき

for a while
I do Tai Chi in a park
near the sea
what a long breath
it requires!

pendant un certain temps
je fait du Tai Chi dans un parc
près de la mer
quel long souffle
cela requiert!

うみちかきそのにひとときまねおれば
umi chikaki sono ni hitotoki mane ore ba

たいきょくけんのいきながかりき
taikyokuken no iki nagakari ki

瀬の音とパンダのかすかな鳴き声の
洩れくる藪に聞き耳立つる

I strain my ears
against a bamboo thicket
and hear
the sound of a stream and
the faint cries of pandas

je tends les oreilles
contre un bosquet de bambous
à partir duquel j'entends
le bruit du ruisseau et
les faibles cris des pandas

せのおととパンダのかすかななきごえの
se no oto to panda no kasukana nakigoe no

もれくるやぶにききみみたつる
more kuru yabu ni kikimimi tatsuru

照る月に湖底の古木息吹きて
立つかとおもふ九寨溝に

in Jiuzhaigou
under the shining moon
the old trees
at the bottom of the lake
seem to breathe and rise

à Jiuzhaigou
sous la lune brillante
les vieux arbres
au fond du lac semblent
respirer et se relever

てるつきにこていのこぼくいきふきて
teru tsuki ni kotei no koboku iki fuki te

たつかとおもうきゅうさいこうに
tatsu ka to omou kyūsaikō ni

第3章
Chapter 3 (2005)

page 38-43 ———— 中国：上海
Shanghai, China
Shanghai, Chine

page 44 ———— インド：ムンバイ
Munbai, India
Mumbai, Inde

page 45-47 ———— ボツワナ
Botswana
Botswana

page 48 ———— 中国：成都
Chengdu, China
Chengdu, Chine

上海の午後はかすかなる日の差して
夕焼もなく闇に入りたり

in Shanghai
the afternoon sun
shines dimly
it's getting dark
without any evening glow

à Shangai
la faible lumière de soleil brille
dans l'après midi
il commence à faire sombre
sans la lueur du crépuscule

しゃんはいのごごはかすかなるひのさして
shanhai no gogo wa kasuka naru hi no sashi te

ゆうやけもなくやみにいりたり
yūyake mo naku yami ni iri tari

夕暮の蘇州外堀めぐりつつ
をりをり仰ぐ寺院の斜塔

＊寒山寺（8世紀頃創建）

at dusk
I walk around the outer moats
in Suzhou
I often stop and look up at
the leaning tower of Han-Shan-Si*

*a temple built around the 8th century

au crépuscule
je marche autour des douves extérieures
à Suzhou
je m'arrête souvent et regarde
la tour penchée du Han-Shan-Si*

*un temple construit à l'environ du 8ème siècle

ゆうぐれのそしゅうそとぼりめぐりつつ
yūgure no soshū sotobori meguri tsutsu

おりおりあおぐじいんのしゃとう
oriori aogu jiin no shatō

城門の外の古き家壊されて
煉瓦の山が風景となる

outside the castle gate
the old houses have been
demolished
a mountain of bricks
forms a landscape

au-delà de la porte du château
de vieilles maisons
sont démolies
une montagne de briques
forme un paysage

じょうもんのそとのふるきやこわされて
jōmon no soto no huruki ya kowasare te

れんがのやまがふうけいとなる
renga no yama ga fūkei to naru

貴国より社会保障は進みたると
言ひて問はるるわれの年金

"our social security
is better than in Japan"
says a Chinese man
and asks me the amount
of my pension

« notre sécurité sociale
est meilleure qu'au Japon »
me dit un Chinois
et me demande le montant
de ma pension

きこくよりしゃかいほしょうはすすみたると
kikoku yori shakai hoshō ga susumi taru to

いいてとわるるわれのねんきん
ii te towa ruru ware no nenkin

夜九時に街灯全て消すと聞く
十三億人の節電対策

I hear that
all streetlights are turned off
at 9:00 pm
it's a power-saving-measure
for 1.3 billion people

j'entends que
tous les lampadaires s' éteignent
à 21h, c'est
pour réduire la consommation électrique
de 1,3 milliard de personnes

よるくじにがいとうすべてけすときく
yoru kuji ni gaitō subete kesu to kiku

じゅうさんおくにんのせつでんたいさく
jūsan oku nin no setsuden taisaku

外灘の夜のはづみのジャズを聴き
蘇州夜曲に涙ぐむわれ

one night
wandering through the Bund
I listen to jazz
Soshu Yakyoku*
moves me to tears

* Suzhou Serenade

errant une nuit
sur les quais à Shanghai
j'écoute du jazz
Soshu Yakyoku*
m'émeut jusqu'aux larme

*Suzhou Sérénade

がいたんのよるのはずみのジャズをきき
gaitan no yoru no hazumi no jazu wo kiki

そしゅうやきょくになみだぐむわれ
soshū yakyoku ni namida gumu ware

牛の背に向けて警笛鳴らしゆけば
左右の群れがすこしづつ空く

passing behind
a herd of cattle
I honk
it gradually diverges
to the right and to the left

passant à l'arrière
d'un troupeau de vaches
je klaxonne
il s'écarte peu à peu
à droite et à gauche

うしのせにむけてけいてきならしゆけば
ushi no se ni muke te keiteki narashi yuke ba

さゆうのむれがすこしずつあく
sayū no mure ga sukoshi zutsu aku

悩み事かかえ込むなと大欠伸
しながら言へり泥水の河馬

giving a big yawn
in muddy water
a hippopotamus
tells me
"don't worry too much"

faisant un gros bâillement
dans l'eau boueuse
un hippopotame
me dit
« ne t'en fait pas trop »

なやみごとかかえこむなとおおあくび
nayami goto kakae komu na to ōakubi

しながらいえりどろみずのかば
shi nagara ie ri doromizu no kaba

アフリカの夕映脳裏に留めむと
象の上よりサバンナを見つ

to keep
the sunset glow in Africa
in my mind
I look over the savannah
from the top of an elephant

pour garder
dans ma mémoire la lueur
du coucher de soleil en Afrique
je regarde la savane
du haut d'un éléphant

アフリカのゆうばえのうりにとどめんと
afurika no yūbae nōri ni todomen to

ぞうのうえよりサバンナをみつ
zō no ue yori sabanna wo mitsu

ささやかな思慕あり西の空指して
くの字の雁が飛びてゆきける

I feel
a kind of longing
wild geese
fly toward the western sky
forming a V-shaped line

j'éprouve
une sorte de nostalgie
les oies sauvages
volent vers le ciel de l'ouest
formant une ligne en V

ささやかなしぼありにしのそらさして
sasayakana shibo ari nishi no sora sashi te

くのじのかりがとびてゆきける
ku no ji no kari ga tobi te yuki keru

好色と思ひつつまねて笑みてみる
川劇*のやや長すぎる笑み

* 中国四川省の古典劇（中国語 Chuānjù）

thinking it's erotic
I smile in the way
of an actor
it's the slightly overlong smile
of the ancient Sichuan opera

pensant que c'est érotique
je souris à la manière
d'un acteur
c'est le sourire un peu trop long
de l' ancien opéra du Sichuan

こうしょくとおもいつつまねてえみてみる
kōshoku to omoi tsutsu mane te emi te miru

せんげきのややながすぎるえみ
sengeki no yaya naga sugiru emi

第4章
Chapter 4 (2006)

page 50-54 ———— ペルー：マチュピチュ
Machu Picchu, Peru
Machu Picchu, Pérou

page 55 ———— 中国：北京
Beijing, China
Pékin, Chine

page 56 ———— チェコ：プラハ
Prague, Czechia
Prague, La Tchéquie

page 57 ———— 中国：成都
Chengdu, China
Chengdu, Chine

page 58-64 ———— 中国：敦煌
Dunhuang, China
Dunhuang, Chine

インカ人とわれとの共通点一つ
酒飲みし翌朝のそつけなさ

I have something
in common with the Incas
the morning after
drinking together
I am quite indifferent

j'ai un point
commun avec les Incas
le lendemain matin
après avoir bu ensemble
je suis assez indifférent

インカびととわれとのきょうつうてんひとつ
inka bito to ware tono kyōtsūten hitotsu

さけのみしよくあさのそっけなさ
sake nomi shi yokuasa no sokkenasa

マチュピチュの巨岩に額すりつけて
呟く死ぬるまで惚けるなと

touching my forehead
to a huge rock of Machu Picchu
I murmur to myself
"until the end of your life
don't ever be senile"

touchant mon front
sur un énorme rocher du Machu Picchu
je me murmure
« jusqu'à la fin de ta vie
ne sois jamais sénile »

マチュピチュのきょがんにひたいすりつけて
machupichu no kyogan ni hitai suri tsuke te

つぶやくしぬるまでぼけるなと
tsubuyaku shinuru made bokeru na to

アミーゴの韻き親しくくり返す
これにて始まる値引き駆引き

amigo
I repeat the tone intimately
it's a formula
to begin bargaining
for discounts

amigo
je répète le ton intimement
c'est une formule
pour commencer
à marchander

アミーゴのひびきしたしくくりかえす
amīgo no hibiki shitashiku kurikaesu

これにてはじまるねびきかけひき
kore nite hajimaru nebiki kakehiki

朝焼は湖のはたてに広がりて
隣国ボリビアの空も明るし

a morning glow
is spreading to the end of the lake
in the adjacent country
the sky over Bolivia
also looks bright

la lueur du matin
s'étend jusqu'au bout du lac
dans le pays voisin
le ciel au-dessus la Bolivie
semble brillant aussi

あさやけはうみのはたてにひろがりて
asayake wa umi no hatate ni hirogari te

りんごくボリビアのそらもあかるし
ringoku boribia no sora mo akaru shi

夕焼は砂丘前方染めあげて
われの背中も輝きをらむ

an evening glow
illuminates the dune
in front of me
my back might
be shining as well

une lueur du soir
éclaire la dune
devant moi
mon dos pourrait
briller aussi

ゆうやけはさきゅうぜんぽうそめあげて
yūyake wa sakyū zenpō someage te

われのせなかもかがやきおらん
ware no senaka mo kagayaki oran

愛人を何と言ふかのわが問ひに
禁止用語とそつけなきガイド

to my question
what is "lover" in Chinese?
my guide
replies on the spot
it's a banned word

à ma question
qu'est-ce que « maîtresse » en chinois?
mon guide
me répond sur le coup
c'est un mot interdit

あいじんをなんというかのわがといに
aijin wo nan to iu ka no waga toi ni

きんしようごとそっけなきガイド
kinshi yōgo to sokkenaki gaido

珈琲を飲まむと茶房に入りたれば
四方の壁にミュシャの美人画

for a coffee
I drop into a tea room
Mucha's paintings
of a pretty woman
hang on four walls

pour un café
je passe au salon de thé
les tableaux de Mucha
d'une jolie femme sont
suspendus au quatre murs

コーヒーをのまんとさぼうにいりたれば
kōhī wo noman to sabō ni iritare ba

しほうのかべにミュシャのびじんが
shihō no kabe ni myusha no bijinga

敦煌のしぐれに濡れて人らみな
両手をかざし夕べの街ゆく

caught in a rain shower
in Dunhuang
all the people go about
with their hands over their heads
in the evening town

pris sous une averse
à Dunhuang
tout le monde s'en va
avec les mains au-dessus de la tête
dans la ville du soir

とんこうのしぐれにぬれてひとらみな
tonkō no shigure ni nure te hito ra mina

りょうてをかざしゆうべのまちゆく
ryōte wo kazashi yūbe no machi yuku

宙に浮くごとく菩薩の描かれて
立ち去れずをり笑みが照らさる

Bodhisattva being depicted
as if floating in the air
I am so fascinated
that I can't leave
the smile is luminous

Bodhisattva étant représenté
comme s'il flottait dans l'air
je suis tellement fasciné
que je ne peux pas m'éloigner
son sourire est illumineux

ちゅうにうくごとくぼさつのえがかれて
chū ni uku gotoku bosatsu no egakare te

たちされずおりえみがてらさる
tachisare zu ori emi ga terasaru

駱駝の背なじまざるまま前脚が
折られて降りる砂原のうへ

the camel's back
doesn't fit me well
the front legs
being folded
I dismount to the desert

le dos du chameau
ne me va pas bien
les pattes de devant
étant repliées
je redescends sur le désert

らくだのせなじまざるまままえあしが
rakuda no se najima zaru mama maeashi ga

おられておりるすなはらのうえ
orare te oriru sunahara no ue

あへぎつつ砂山のぼり振向けば
影をともなふ月牙泉*の綺羅

* 三日月形の泉、中国甘粛省敦煌

out of breath
after climbing the dune
I turn around and see
the silky spring of the Yue Ya Quan*
accompanied by shadow

* the Crescent Lake, spring in the form of crescent, Dunhuang, Gansu, in China

hors d'haleine
après avoir escaladé la dune
je me retoune et vois
la source soyeuse du Yue Ya Quan*
accompagnée d'ombre

*le Lac du Croissant, source en forme de croissant, Dunhuang, Gansu, en Chine

あえぎつつすなやまのぼりふりむけば
aegi tsutsu sunayama nobori huri muke ba

かげをともなうげつがせんのきら
kage wo tomonau getsugasen no kira

黄塵のかげ更けにける鳴沙山*
前行く人の吐く息聞こゆ

* 鳴き砂の砂丘、中国甘粛省月牙山の近郊

at Ming Sha Shan*
the shadow of yellow dust
stretches further
I even hear the breath of
the people ahead of me

*the Singing Sand Dunes, near Yue Ya Quan

à Ming Sha Shan*
l'ombre de poussières jaunes
s'allonge encore plus
j'entends même le souffle
des gens devant

* les « Dunes qui chantent » près du Yue Ya Quan

こうじんのかげふけにけるめいさざん
kōjin no kage fuke ni keru meisazan

まえゆくひとのはくいききこゆ
mae yuku hito no haku iki kikoyu

経典を記す幟がはためきて
鳥葬なればたましひは空

banners with sutras
flap in the wind
the corpses
are left to the vultures
their souls rest in the sky

des bannières de sutras
claquent au vent
les cadavres
sont laissés aux vautours
leurs âmes reposent au ciel

きょうてんをしるすのぼりがはためきて
kyōten wo shirusu nobori ga hatameki te

ちょうそうなればたましいはそら
chōsō nare ba tamashii wa sora

頂きにしかばねを刻む鳥葬師
文化違へどかなしみに満つ

on the mountain top
the undertaker chops up
a corpse for the vultures
the culture is different
but I am filled with grief

au sommet de la montagne
le croque-mort hache
un cadavre pour les vautours
la culture est différente
mais je suis rempli de chagrin

いただきにしかばねをきざむちょうそうし
itadaki ni shikabane wo kizamu chōsō shi

ぶんかたがえどかなしみにみつ
bunka tagae do kanashimi ni mitsu

第5章
Chapter 5 (2007-2008)

page 66 ———— マレーシア：クアラルンプール
Kuala Lumpur, Malasia
Kuala Lumpur, Malaisie

page 67-69 ———— ブラジル：アマゾン
Amazon, Brasil
Amazon, Brésil

page 70-73 ———— カンボジア：アンコール・ワット
Angkor Wat, Cambodia
Angkor Vat, Cambodge

page 74-75 ———— 中国：桂林
Guilin, China
Guilin, Chin

page 76 ———— ロシア：モスクワ
Moscow, Russia
Moscou, Russie

page 77-78 ———— ロシア：イルクーツク
Irkutsk, Russia
Irkutsk, Russie

page 79-81 ———— ロシア：バイカル湖
lake Baikal, Russia
le lac Baïkal, Russie

をさな等が踏み場なきほど溢れゐて
密林に住む長と握手す

the venue
overflowing with children
without room to move
I shake hands with their chief
who lives in the jungle

le lieu
débordant d'enfants
sans place pour bouger
je serre la main de leur chef
qui vit dans la jungle

おさならがふみばなきほどあふれいて
osana ra ga humiba naki hodo afure ite

みつりんにすむおさとあくしゅす
mitsurin ni sumu osa to akushu su

アマゾンのピラニア喰ふてふ広告に
参加を決めたる俳句の旅へ

induced by
the ad stating we'll eat
Amazonian piranha
I decide to join
the Haiku tour

induit par la pub
disant que nous mangerons
des piranhas amazoniens
je décide de rejoindre
la tournée de Haïku

アマゾンのピラニアくうちょうこうこくに
amazon no pirania kū chou kōkoku ni

さんかをきめたるはいくのたびへ
sanka wo kime taru haiku no tabi e

晴れわたる滝の真中に虹立ちて
イグアス全体地響きと化す

it's sunny
a rainbow appears in the middle
of the waterfall
all of Iguazú becomes
a grumble of earth tremors

Il fait beau
un arc-en-ciel apparaît au milieu
de la cascade
l'Iguazú au complet devient
des grondements séismiques

はれわたるたきのまなかににじたちて
harewataru taki no manaka ni niji tachi te

イグアスぜんたいじひびきとかす
iguasu zentai jihibiki to kasu

アマゾンの蝶が天より溢れ来て
あたりたちまち光のしぐれ

Amazonian butterflies
have overflowed
from heaven
I then find myself
under a shower of lights

les papillons amazoniens
ont débordé
du paradis
je me retrouve alors
sous une pluie de lumières

アマゾンのちょうがてんよりあふれきて
amazon no chō ga ten yori afure ki te

あたりたちまちひかりのしぐれ
atari tachimachi hikari no shigure

痩せぎすの犬が飲みゐる池の水
アンコールワットの塔が映れり

an emaciated dog
drinks water of a moat
in Angkor Wat
the tower of the temple
is reflected on the surface

un chien émacié
boit l'eau d'un fossé
à Angkor Vat
la tour du temple
se reflète sur la surface

やせぎすのいぬがのみいるいけのみず
yasegisu no inu ga nomi iru ike no mizu

アンコールワットのとうがうつれり
ankōruwatto no tō ga utsure ri

好き嫌い好きと二匹の蝶が舞ふ
女神の像の耳たぶのそば

you love me, a little,
a lot, not at all, you love me
two butterflies flutter
around the earlobe
of the statue of the goddess

tu m'aimes, un peu,
beaucoup, pas du tout, tu m'aimes
deux papillons voltigent
autour du lobe de l'oreille
de la statue de la déesse

すききらいすきとにひきのちょうがまう
suki kirai suki to ni hiki no chō ga mau

めがみのぞうのみみたぶのそば
megami no zō no mimitabu no soba

四百年経たるガジュマルの長き根が
回廊抱く大蛇のごとく

a long root
of the 400-year-old banyan tree
twines
around the gallery
like a giant snake

la longue racine
du banian vieux de 400 ans
s'enroule
autour de la galerie
comme un serpent géant

よんひゃくねんへたるガジュマルのながきねが
yon hyaku nen hetaru gajumaru no nagaki ne ga

かいろういだくおろちのごとく
kairō idaku orochi no gotoku

夕日見むと遺跡の丘にのぼり来て
声なく坐る人なかに居る

going up
the hill of ruins
to enjoy the sunset
I find myself sitting calmly
within a crowd

montant
la colline des ruines
pour admirer le couchant
je me retrouve assis calmement
au sein d'une foule

ゆうひみんといせきのおかにのぼりきて
yūhi min to iseki no oka ni nobori ki te

こえなくすわるひとなかにいる
koe naku suwaru hitonaka ni iru

窓越しに売り子の扇子の数増えて
千円千円の声潤みくる

a sales woman
increasing the number of folding fans
shouts in a tear-choked voice
through the window of a train
"1,000 yen! 1,000 yen!"

une vendeuse
augmentant le nombre d'éventails
crie par la fenêtre d'un train
sa voix étranglée de larmes
« 1,000 yen! 1,000 yen! »

まどごしにうりこのせんすのかずふえて
madogoshi ni uriko no sensu no kazu fue te

せんえんせんえんのこえうるみくる
sen en sen en no koe urumi kuru

たそがれて顔おぼろなる出稼ぎ者
暗き屋台のどんぶり啜る

in the twilight
a migrant worker's face
is hazy
the sound of slurping from a bowl
echoes from the dark food stand

au crépuscule
le visage d'un travailleur migrant
est flou
on entend gober un bol de nourriture
dans un kiosque alimentaire sombre

たそがれてかおおぼろなるでかせぎしゃ
tasogare te kao oboro naru dekasegi sha

くらきやたいのどんぶりすする
kuraki yatai no donburi susuru

瑞々しく口に広ごるモスクワの
かけがへのなき真冬の胡瓜

fresh and juicy
the taste of cucumbers
spreads in the mouth
it's a precious flavour
of Moscow in Winter

frais et juteux
le goût de concombres se diffuse
dans la bouche
c'est une saveur précieuse
de Moscou en hiver

みずみずしくくちにひろごるモスクワの
mizumizushiku kuchi ni hirogoru mosukuwa no

かけがえのなきまふゆのきゅうり
kakegae no naki mafuyu no kyūri

黄緑の炎生きものさながらに
星を透かして覆ふオーロラ

yellow-green flames
spirited like living beings
the aurora
transparently covers
a starry sky

des flammes jaune-vert
s'animent comme
des êtres vivants
en transparence l'aurore
recouvre un ciel étoilé

きみどりのほのおいきものさながらに
kimidori no honō ikimono sanagara ni

ほしをすかしておおうオーロラ
hoshi wo sukashi te ōu ōrora

全天のオーロラわれに降りそそぐ
長く生き来て呆けし顔に

the aurora
across the entire sky
pours its light on me
onto my senile face
I have lived a long time

l'aurore
dans tout le ciel
me verse sa lumière
sur le visage sénile
je vis depuis longtemps

ぜんてんのオーロラわれにふりそそぐ
zenten no ōrora ware ni furi sosogu

ながくいききてほうけしかおに
nagaku iki kite hōke shi kao ni

本名をあばら骨のごと卒塔婆に
印さるシベリア抑留者の墓

real names of the deceased
are written on the stupas
like ribs
it's a graveyard
of the detainees in Siberia

les vrais noms de défunts
sont écrits sur les stupas
comme des côtes
c'est un cimetière
des détenus en Sibérie

ほんみょうをあばらぼねのごとそとうばに
honmyō wo abarabone no goto sotōba ni

しるさるシベリアよくりゅうしゃのはか
shirusaru shiberia yokuryū sha no haka

二千万人のロシアの民が死にしとふ
日本兵抑留の大戦の裏

I hear that
twenty million Russians died
Japanese soldiers
were detained in Siberia
after World War II

j'entends que
vingt millions de russes sont morts
des soldats japonais
ont été détenus en Sibérie
après la Deuxième Guerre mondiale

にせんまんにんのロシアのたみがしにしとう
nisen man nin no rosia no tami ga shini shi tou

にほんへいよくりゅうのたいせんのうら
nihonhei yokuryū no taisen no ura

抑留者の霊が湖底に手繰り寄す
招きのごとし船尾の揺れは

the stern of the boat
rolls and pitches
it seems to me
an invitation of the detainees' souls
to the bottom of the lake

la poupe du bateau
roule et tangue
il me semble
une invitation au fond du lac
des âmes des détenus

よくりゅうしゃのれいがこていにたぐりよす
yokuryū sha no rei ga kotei ni taguri yosu

まねきのごとしせんびのゆれは
maneki no gotoshi senbi no yure wa

第6章
Chapter 6 (2009-2010)

page 84-86 ——— ネパール：カトマンズ
Katmandu, Nepal
Katmandou, Népal

page 87-89 ——— 台湾：台北
Taipei, Taiwan
Taipei, Taïwan

敷きつめて屋根に干したる子どもらの
下着かがやく路地の孤児院

children's underwear
spread all over the roof
shines as it dries
it's the orphanage
in the alley

des sous-vêtements d'enfants
étendus partout sur le toit
brillent en séchant
c'est l'orphelinat
dans la ruelle

しきつめてやねにほしたるこどもらの
shiki tsume te yane ni hoshi taru kodomo ra no

したぎかがやくろじのこじいん
shitagi kagayaku roji no kojiin

山襞に湧きたる霧がヒマラヤの
山小屋包みわれらをおほふ

the fog
springing from mountain folds
envelopes
the Himalayan hut
as well as us inside

le brouillard
jaillissant des plis de la montagne
enveloppe
la cabane himalayenne
ainsi que nous à l'intérieur

やまひだにわきたるきりがヒマラヤの
yama hida ni waki taru kiri ga himaraya no

やまごやつつみわれらをおおう
yamagoya tsutsumi ware ra wo ōu

生きゆくてふ問ひを続ける日々ありし
ヒマラヤ連峰たそがれんとす

I recall the days
when I repeatedly asked myself
what is life?
twilight is approaching
in the Himalayas

je me rappelle des jours
où je continuais à me poser la question
qu'est-ce que la vie?
le crépuscule s'approche
dans l'Himalaya

いきゆくちょうといをつづけるひびありし
iki yuku chou toi wo tsuzukeru hibi arishi

ヒマラヤれんぽうたそがれんとす
himaraya renpō tasogaren to su

喧騒の夜の市のなかパスポート
胸にたしかめ満月あふぐ

in the hustle and bustle
of the night market
I check
that my passport is on me
I look up at the full moon

dans l'agitation
du marché nocturne
je vérifie
que mon passeport est avec moi
je regarde la pleine lune

けんそうのよのいちのなかパスポート
kensō no yo no ichi no naka pasupōto

むねにたしかめまんげつあおぐ
mune ni tashikame mangetsu aogu

隊伍組み歩調合せてゆく兵の
靴底鋲のしばしばひかる

soldiers
are marching on parade
metal fittings
under the soles of their shoes
sometimes glitter

les soldats
défilent en parade
les ferrures métalliques
sous la semelle de leurs chaussures
brillent parfois

たいごくみほちょうあわせてゆくへいの
taigo kumi hochō awase te yuku hei no

くつぞこびょうのしばしばひかる
kutsuzoko byō no shibashiba hikaru

瞬きをせぬ兵なれどその頬に
赤みのありてわれは親しむ

a soldier
is unblinking
however, I feel
sympathy for him
because of the redness of his cheeks

un soldat
ne cligne pas des yeux
toutefois j'éprouve
de la sympathie pour lui
à cause de la rougeur de ses joues

またたきをせぬへいなれどそのほほに
mabataki wo senu hei naredo sono hoho ni

あかみのありてわれはしたしむ
akami no ari te ware wa shitashimu

第7章
Chapter 7 （20011-2012）

page 92 ———— 米国：シアトル
Seattle, USA
Seattle, les États-Unis

page 93-95 ———— フィリピン：マニラ
Manila, Philipppines
Manille, Philipppines

page 96 ———— ボスニア・ヘルツェゴヴィナ：サラエボ
Sarajevo, Bosnia & Herzegovina
Sarajevo, Bosnie-Herzégovine

page 97-100 ———— 韓国：釜山
Pusan, the Republic of Korea
Pusan, République de Corée

page 101-103 ———— カンボジア：プノンペン
Phnom Penh, Cambodia
Phnom Penh, Cambodge

震災の支援感謝の幕持ちて
われらはすすむシアトルの街

holding a banner
to show our gratitude for the support
after the Earthquake*
we paraded down
the street in Seattle

*The Great East Japan Earthquake, March 11, 2011

tenant une bannière
pour montrer notre gratitude pour le soutien
après le séisme*
nous avons défilé
dans la rue à Seattle

* le grand séisme de l'est du Japon, le 11 mars, 2011

しんさいのしえんかんしゃのまくもちて
shinsai no shien kansha no maku mochi te

われらはすすむシアトルのまち
ware ra wa susumu shiatoru no machi

要塞の刑場までのリサール*の
足跡のうへを踏みてあゆめり

* フィリピン独立運動の初期の指導者（1861-1896）

retracing the footsteps
of José Rizal* to the place of execution
in the fortress
I walk the path
of his final moment

*Filipino patriot (1861-1896)

retraçant les pas
de José Rizal * au lieu d'exécution
dans la forteresse
je parcours le chemin
de son dernier moment

* patriote philippin (1861-1896)

ようさいのけいじょうまでのリサールの
yōsai no keijō made no risāru no

あしあとのうえをふみてあゆめり
ashiato no ue wo fumi te ayume ri

日雇の仕事なくなり子どもらの
稼ぐ駄賃にて暮らしゐるといふ

a day labourer
having lost his job
for subsistence, he says
he relies on the bit of money
his children earn on the street

un journalier
ayant perdu son emploi
pour la subsistance
il dit compter sur le peu d'argent
gagné par ses enfants dans la rue

ひやといのしごとなくなりこどもらの
hiyatoi no shigoto nakunari kodomo ra no

かせぐだちんにてくらしいるという
kasegu dachin nite kurashi iru to iu

肩書の一つに「銃の製造」と
刷りたる名刺ライオンズマンより

"gun-manufacturing"
is one of the jobs printed
on the business card
I received from
a member of the Lions Club

« fabrication d'armes à feu »
est l'un des metiers imprimés
sur la carte de visite
que j'ai reçu
d'un membre du Lions Club

かたがきのひとつに「じゅうのせいぞう」と
katagaki no hitotsu ni "jū no seizō" to

すりたるめいしライオンズマンより
suri taru meishi raionzu man yori

真向ひの道をはさみて殺し合ふ
それが内戦とセルビア人言ふ

neighbors
on either side of the street
kill each other
this is our civil war
says a Serb

les voisins
de part et d'autre de la rue
s'entre-tuent
c'est notre guerre civile
dit un Serbe

まむかいのみちをはさみてころしあう
mamukai no michi wo hasami te koroshi au

それがないせんとセルビアじんいう
sore ga naisen to serubia jin iu

地下鉄の乗換駅にて迷ひたる
われをみちびく釜山の翁は

I get lost
in the subway transfer station
an old gentleman in Busan
shows me the way
to the right place

je me perds
dans la station de transfert du métro
un vieux monsieur à Busan
me montre le chemin
vers le bon endroit

ちかてつののりかええきにてまよいたる
chikatetsu no norikae eki nite mayoi taru

われをみちびくぷさんのおきなは
ware wo michibiku pusan no okina wa

穏やかなる日本語聞けば忘れたる
優しきこころ拾へる如し

listening to a Korean
softly speaking Japanese
it seems to me
that I regain the warm heart
I had forgotten

écoutant un Coréen
parler doucement le japonais
il me semble
que je retrouve le cœur chaud
que j'avais oublié

おだやかなるにほんごきけばわすれたる
odayaka naru nihongo kike ba wasure taru

やさしきこころひろえるごとし
yasashiki kokoro hiroeru gotoshi

韓国の金井山麓の径に佇つ
われの祖先を思ひなどして

standing on the path
at the foot of Mt. Kanai*
in South Korea
I think of my ancestors
and so on

*the Geumjeong Mountain

debout sur le sentier
au pied du mont Kanaï*
en Corée du Sud
je pense à mes ancêtres
et cetera

* la montagne de Geumjeong

かんこくのかないさんろくのみちにたつ
kankoku no kanai sanroku no michi ni tatsu

われのそせんをおもいなどして
ware no sosen wo omoi nado shite

ずんぐりと建ちて山風なつかしき
新羅時代の梵魚寺*の門は

*西暦678年創建

in a mountain breeze
the sturdy entry gates
to Beomeosa temple*
built in the Silla era
make me feel nostalgic

*established in A.D.678

dans une brise de montagne
les portes robustes
du Temple Beomeosa*
construit à l'époque de Silla
me rendent nostalgique

*établi en A.D.678

ずんぐりとたちてやまかぜなつかしき
zunguri to tachi te yamakaze natsukashiki

しらぎじだいのぼんぎょじのもんは
shiragi jidai no bongyoji no mon wa

どれほどの命かと問ふ母を置き
プノンペンへ発つ富士の夕焼

leaving behind my mother
who asks how long she could live
I depart to Phnom Penh
Mount Fuji looks
aglow at sunset

laissant derrière ma mère
qui demande combien de temps elle pourrait vivre
je pars pour Phnom Penh
le mont Fuji s'illumine
au coucher du soleil

どれほどのいのちかととうははをおき
dore hodo no inochi ka to tou haha wo oki

プノンペンへたつふじのゆうやけ
punonpen e tatsu fuji no yūyake

義太夫のテレビを観つつたひらかに
母死にたりしと電話かかり来

an emergency call
my mother has passed away
peacefully
watching TV — a recital
of her favorite gidayu*

*the traditional Japanese art of storytelling with music and puppets

un appel d'urgence
ma mère est décédée
paisiblement
en regardant à la télé un récital
de son gidayu* préféré

*l'art traditionnel japonais de narration d'un conte avec de la musique et des marionnettes

ぎだゆうのテレビをみつつたいらかに
gidayū no terebi wo mitsutsu tairaka ni

ははしにたりしとでんわかかりく
haha shini tari shi to denwa kakari ku

日頃より自立してゐし母の死は
わが行程に支障きたさず

my mother
was always so independent
that her death
doesn't interfere at all
with my itinerary

ma mère
était toujours si indépendante
que sa mort
ne dérange aucunement
mon itinéraire

ひごろよりじりつしていしははのしは
higoro yori jiritsu shite i shi haha no shi wa

わがこうていにししょうきたさず
waga kōtei ni shishō kitasa zu

第8章
Chapter 8 (2013-2014)

page 106-110 ── ベトナム
Vietnam
Viêt Nam

page 111 ── ドイツ：ベルリン
Berlin, Germany
Berlin, Allemagne

page 112-119 ── モンゴル
Mongolia
Mongolie

page 120 ── バチカン市国：サン・ピエトロ
Saint Peter's Basilica, Vatican
Basilique Saint-Pierre, Vatican

首のなき菩薩の列に降りそそぐ
日差はベトナム五月の太陽

on a row
of headless
stone Bodhisattvas
the May sun
shines in Vietnam

sur une rangée
de Bodhisattva en pierre
sans tête
le soleil de mai
brille au Viêt Nam

くびのなきぼさつのれつにふりそそぐ
kubi no naki bosatsu no retsu ni furi sosogu

ひざしはベトナムごがつのたいよう
hizashi wa betonamu gogatsu no taiyō

緑濁のフォン川下りの商ひに
匍匐前進なす玩具あり

going down
the muddy-green Huong River*
I saw a peddler
selling toys that crawl
to move forward

*Sông Huong: the Perfume River

en descendant
la Huong*, rivière verte et boueuse
j'ai vu un colporteur
vendre des jouets qui
avancent en rampant

*Sông Huong: la rivière des Parfums

りょくだくのフォンがわくだりのあきないに
ryokudaku no fon gawa kudari no akinai ni

ほふくぜんしんなすおもちゃあり
hohuku zenshin nasu omocha ari

僧坊に法衣をあらふ少年の
声透きとほる青葉を抜けて

the voice of a boy who
washes the monks' robes
in the dormitory
passes transparently
among fresh green leaves

la voix d'un garçon qui
lave les robes des bonzes
dans le dortoir
passe en toute transparence
à travers les feuilles vertes

そうぼうにほうえをあらうしょうねんの
sōbō ni hōe wo arau shōnen no

こえすきとおるあおばをぬけて
koe sukitōru aoba wo nukete

アオザイを纏ふ女につくごとく
つかざるが如く橋を渡れり

as if unsure
as to whether or not
I want to follow
a woman wearing áo dài*
I cross the bridge

*traditional Vietnamese garment

comme si je n'étais pas sûr
de vouloir ou de ne pas vouloir
suivre
une femme portant un áo dài*
je traverse le pont

*costume traditionnel au Viêt Nam

アオザイをまとうおんなにつくごとく
aozai wo matou on'na ni tsuku gotoku

つかざるがごとくはしをわたれり
tsuka zaru ga gotoku hashi wo watare ri

ビルの長きネオン映せるサイゴン川
昏き流れの水草はやし

the Saigon River
reflects long neon lights
of buildings
water plants are rippling
in the dark current

la rivière de Saïgon
reflète les longs néons
des bâtiments
des plantes d'eau ondulent
dans le courant sombre

ビルのながきネオンうつせるサイゴンがわ
biru no nagaki neon utsuseru saigon gawa

くらきながれのみずくさはやし
kuraki nagare no mizukusa hayashi

この館にてポツダム宣言せしといふ
庭に芙蓉の大きく咲き満つ

in this palace
the Potsdam Declaration
was proclaimed
large mallows in the garden
are in full bloom

dans ce palais
la déclaration de Potsdam
a été proclamée
de grandes mauves dans le jardin
sont en pleine floraison

このやかたにてポツダムせんげんせしという
kono yakata nite potsudamu sengen seshi to iu

にわにふようのおおきくさきみつ
niwa ni fuyō no ōkiku saki mitsu

タイヤ一つころがす子のあと三人の
幼な蹤きゆく草原傾り

three children
follow the child who
rolls a tire
on the slope of
the grassland

un enfant
roule un pneu
trois autres
le suivent sur la pente
de la prairie

タイヤひとつころがすこのあとさんにんの
taiya hitotsu korogasu ko no ato san nin no

おさなつきゆくそうげんなだり
osana tsuki yuku sōgen nadari

渓あひに羊群がりをりをりに
手を翳し見るゲルの老婆は

an old woman of the yurt
sometimes shades her face
with her hand
better to see the flock
of sheep in the valley

une vieille de la yourte
ombrage parfois son visage
d'une main
pour mieux voir le troupeau
de moutons dans la vallée

たにあいにひつじむらがりおりおりに
taniai ni hitsuji muragari oriori ni

てをかざしみるゲルのろうばは
te wo kazashi miru geru no rōba wa

自らの力にて生きて来たりしと
威厳に満ちたる老婆の言葉

I've managed
to live by my own strength
says an old woman
her words are
full of dignity

j'ai réussi
à vivre de mes propres forces
dit une vieille femme
ses mots sont
pleins de dignité

みずからのちからにていきてきたりしと
mizukara no chikara nite ikite kitari shi to

いげんにみちたるろうばのことば
igen ni michi taru rōba no kotoba

わが乗りしモンゴル馬は歩まずに
疎らなる草さがすに夢中

the Mongolian horse
I'm riding
doesn't walk
being absorbed in
its search for sparse grass

le cheval mongol
que je monte
ne marche pas
il est absorbé
par sa quête d'herbes rares

わがのりしモンゴルうまはあゆまずに
wa ga nori shi mongoru uma wa ayuma zu ni

まばらなるくささがすにむちゅう
mabara naru kusa sagasu ni muchū

乾きたる家畜の糞を炉に焼べば
薬草の香ぞ辺りに満つる

I'm burning
the dried dung of livestock
in the fireplace
the smell of medicinal herbs
fills the room in our yurt

dans la cheminée
je brûle le crottin séché
du bétail
l'odeur des herbes médicinales
remplit la pièce de notre yourte

かわきたるかちくのふんをろにくべば
kawaki taru kachiku no fun wo ro ni kube ba

やくそうのかぞあたりにみつる
yakusō no ka zo atari ni mitsuru

火力発電の黒煙帯なす街に覚め
集合住宅脇にゲル見ゆ

I wake up in town
under a band of black smoke
from a thermal power plant
yurts are visible
next to modern apartments

je me réveille en ville
sous une bande de fumée noire
d'une centrale thermique
on voit des yourtes à côté
d'appartements modernes

かりょくはつでんのこくえんおびなすまちにさめ
karyoku hatsuden no kokuen obi nasu machi ni same

しゅうごうじゅうたくわきにゲルみゆ
shūgō jūtaku waki ni geru miyu

七千メートル以下の山の名記されぬ
地図を購ふ UlanBator

names of mountains
under 7,000-meters in height
are not indicated
I bought a map
in Ulaanbaatar

on n'indique pas
les noms des montagnes ayant
moins de 7000 mètres de haut
j'ai acheté une carte
à Oulan-Bator

ななせんメートルいかのやまのなしるされぬ
nana sen mētoru ika no yama no na shirusare nu

ちずをあがなうウランバートル
chizu wo aganau uranbātoru

日本人千七百余の兵眠る
墓地ありウランバートルの街なか

there is
a cemetery in the city of
Ulaanbaatar
where about 1,700
Japanese soldiers sleep

Il y a
un cimetière dans la ville
d'Oulan-Bator
où dorment environ
1700 soldats japonais

にほんじんせんななひゃくよのへいねむる
nihonjin sen nana hyaku yo no hei nemuru

ぼちありウランバートルのまちなか
bochi ari uranbātoru no machinaka

水色の衣のをみなの寄りて来て
去りたるあとに札入れ失せし

a lady
in a light blue dress comes up to me
and leaves
and then my wallet
is also gone

une dame
en robe bleu clair s'approche de moi
et s'éloigne
et puis mon portefeuille
est aussi parti

みずいろのころもものおみなのよりてきて
mizuiro no koromo no omina no yori te ki te

さりたるあとにさついれうせし
sari taru ato ni satsuire use shi

120

第9章
Chapter 9 (2015-2016)

page 122-126 ———— ブータン
Bhutan
Bhoutan

page 127-128 ———— インド
India
Inde

にっぽんの西岡京治の指導せし
棚田は壮大胸あつく見き

the terraced rice field
as taught by Keiji Nishioka
of Japan
is magnificent—to see it
warms my heart

la rizière en terrasse
tel qu'enseignée par Keiji Nishioka
du Japon
est magnifique – la voir
me réchauffe le cœur

にっぽんのにしおかけいじのしどうせし
nippon no nishioka keiji no shidō seshi

たなだはそうだいむねあつくみき
tanada wa sōdai mune atsuku mi ki

標高七千チョモラリの雪かがやける
三角峯に朝日のぼり来

at a height of 7,000 meters
the snow on Mount Jomolhari
shines
the morning sun is rising
on a triangular peak

à 7 000 mètres d'altitude
la neige sur le mont Chomolhari
brille
le soleil du matin se lève
sur un sommet triangulaire

ひょうこうななせんチョモラリのゆきかがやける
hyōkō nana sen chomorari no yuki kagayakeru

さんかくみねにあさひのぼりく
sankaku mine ni asahi nobori ku

山脈がブータン国を守りしか
首都取り囲む道の険しさ

do the mountain ranges
provide Bhutan
with protection?
the capital is surrounded
by steep roads

les chaînes de montagnes
protègent-elles
le Bhoutan?
la capitale est entourée
par des chemins escarpés

さんみゃくがブータンこくをまもりしか
sanmyaku ga būtan koku wo mamorishi ka

しゅととりかこむみちのけわしさ
shuto torikakomu michi no kewashisa

木の床に足のかたちの窪みあり
五体投地もて祈れる寺院

I pray
prostrate on the temple's
parquet floor
there are footprints
worn into the wood

je prie
prosterné sur le parquet
du temple
il y a des traces de pieds
empreintes dans le bois

きのゆかにあしのかたちのくぼみあり
ki no yuka ni ashi no katachi no kubomi ari

ごたいとうちもていのれるじいん
gotaitōchi mote inoreru jiin

数多ゐる露店の筵の蛙にも
仏性こもるかブータンならば

so many frogs
on a straw mat
in the street stall
would they have Buddha nature
because they live in Bhutan?

bien des grenouilles
sur un tapis de paille
dans l'étal de rue
auraient-elles la nature de bouddha
parce qu'elles vivent au Bhoutan?

あまたいるろてんのむしろのかえるにも
amata iru roten no mushiro no kaeru ni mo

ぶっしょうこもるかブータンならば
busshō komoru ka būtan naraba

夕日見る人の多さに慣れながら
立つ位置さがす海への石段

getting used to the crowds
who watch the sunset
I search for a spot
on the stone steps
leading to the ocean

m'habituant à la foule
qui regarde le soleil couchant
je cherche une place
sur les marches de pierre
menant à l'océan

ゆうひみるひとのおおさになれながら
yūhi miru hito no ōsa ni nare nagara

たついちさがすうみへのいしだん
tatsu ichi sagasu umi e no ishidan

仏壇に白黒赤茶の砂供ふ
アラビア・印度・ベンガル湾の砂

at the Buddhist altar
I offer white, black, red,
and brown sand
brought back from Arabia, India,
and the Bay of Bengal

à l'autel bouddhiste
j'offre du sable blanc, noir, rouge
et brun
ramené de l'Arabie, de l'Inde
et du golfe du Bengale

ぶつだんにしろくろあかちゃのすなそなう
butsudan ni shiro kuro aka cha no suna sonau

アラビア・インド・ベンガルわんのすな
arabia · indo · bengaru wan no suna

第10章
Chapter 10 （2017-2018）

page 130-131 ──── ロシア：サハリン
Sakhalin, Russia
Sakhaline, Russie

page 132-134 ──── スリランカ
Sri Lanka
Sri Lanka

page 135 ──── 米国：ラスベガス
Las Vegas, USA
Las Vegas, les États-Unis

page 136-137 ──── 米国：グランドキャニオン
Grand Canyon, USA
Grand Canyon, les États-Unis

王子製紙工場跡のヤナギラン
雑草覆ふその上に咲く

at the ruins
of the Oji paper mill
fireweed
is blooming
among the weeds

aux ruines
de l'usine de papier Oji
des épilobes
fleurissent
parmi les mauvaises herbes

おうじせいしこうじょうあとのやなぎらん
ōjiseishi kōjō ato no yanagiran

ざっそうおおうそのうえにさく
zassō ōu sono ue ni saku

サハリンの山に戦ひの兵埋めし
墳墓あまたに寄り添ふ白樺

dead soldiers
are buried on the mountain
in Sakhalin
white birch trees grow
as if embracing all these tombs

des soldats morts
sont enterrés dans la montagne
de Sakhaline
des bouleaux blancs poussent
comme s'ils gardaient toutes ces tombes

サハリンのやまにたたかいのへいうめし
saharin no yama ni tatakai no hei umeshi

ふんぼあまたによりそうしらかば
hunbo amata ni yorisou shirakaba

賽銭のルピー硬貨がするすると
釈迦の台座に当たりて止まる

a rupee coin
tossed as an offering
rolls smoothly
then stops as it hits
the pedestal of the Buddha

une pièce de roupie
jetée en offrande
roule en douceur
puis s'arrête en frappant
le socle du Bouddha

さいせんのルピーこうかがするすると
saisen no rupī kōka ga surusuru to

しゃかのだいざにあたりてとまる
shaka no daiza ni atari te tomaru

空爆に逃げ惑ひしと内戦を
語るガイドのひとこと重し

even a word
about the civil war is heavy
the guide says
"the airstrikes had us fleeing
pell-mell every which way"

un mot même
sur la guerre civile est lourd
le guide dit
« les raids aériens nous faisaient
fuir pêle-mêle en tous sens »

くうばくににげまどいしとないせんを
kūbaku ni nige madoishi to naisen wo

かたるガイドのひとことおもし
kataru gaido no hitokoto omoshi

まぼろしの時空に浸る酒を得し
釈迦の足跡巡りし夜は

at night, after the tour
to follow Buddha's footsteps
I get some liquor
and soak in
the spacetime of reverie

la nuit, après le tour
pour suivre les pas de Bouddha
je prends de l'alcool
et me trempe dans
l'espace-temps de la reverie

まぼろしのじくうにひたるさけをえし
maboroshi no jikū ni hitaru sake wo e shi

しゃかのあしあとめぐりしよるは
shaka no ashiato meguri shi yoru wa

絶叫のジェットコースター付きホテル
妻のみ乗りにゆかせて待てり

letting
my wife go alone
on the hotel's
scary roller coaster
I wait for her

en laissant
ma femme monter seule
dans les effrayantes
montagnes russes de l' hôtel
je l'attends

ぜっきょうのジェットコースターつきホテル
zekkyō no jettokōsutā tsuki hoteru

つまのみのりにゆかせてまてり
tsuma nomi nori ni yukase te materi

キャニオンの左右の幅は東京から
名古屋までなりアイスを舐める

from right to left
the width of the Grand Canyon
is equal to the distance
from Tokyo to Nagoya
I lick an ice cream cone

de droite à gauche
la largeur du Grand Canyon
est égale à la distance
de Tokyo à Nagoya
je lèche un cornet de glace

キャニオンのさゆうのはばはとうきょうから
kyanion no sayū no haba wa tōkyō kara

なごやまでなりアイスをなめる
nagoya made nari aisu wo nameru

千メートルの深さに千の層成して
グランドキャニオン日暮れてゆきぬ

formed of a thousand layers
to a depth of a thousand meters
the Grand Canyon
is growing dark
night is gradually falling

formé de mille couches
jusqu'à une profondeur
de mille mètres
le Grand Canyon devient sombre
la nuit tombe petit à petit

せんメートルのふかさにせんのそうなして
sen mētoru no fukasa ni sen no sō nashi te

グランドキャニオンひぐれてゆきぬ
gurando kyanion higurete yuki nu

訳者あとがき

　金井一夫氏の第一歌集『海外詠』を手にしたのは、2019年12月でした。一読して、その視野の広さと洞察の深さに衝撃を受けました。これは日本の歌人のみならず、海外の歌人にも大きな反響と感動を呼び起こすに違いないと感じました。直ちに、『海外詠』から3首を選んで英語と仏語に翻訳しました。そして、2020年5月1日発行の *INTERNATIONAL TANKA* 第7号に投稿しました。

　2021年夏、同誌を目にされた金井一夫氏が我が家を訪問され、自選112首の翻訳を依頼されました。私は快諾しました。何故なら、日本人が外国を訪問して短歌を詠み、それを外国語に翻訳して日本から発信することは、外国の読者が「自分自身について理解を深める」ことに貢献すると思ったからです。その結果実現したこの翻訳歌集は、日本人の目を以って、鏡の如く、外国文化を世界に反射しているように思われます。

　デカルトは「われ考ふ、故に、われ在り」といいました。これは間違っていないと思います。しかし、自分自身を客観的に理解するには、更にもう一つの思考プロセス、即ち「汝考ふ、故に、われ在り」の検証が必要です。本歌集は、その役割を担っています。

　最後に、英語については米国ワシントン州のYukiko Inoue Smith氏、仏語に関しては千葉のFabrice Alessandro氏、英語と仏語及び全体の監修についてはカナダ・モントリオールのMaxianne Berger氏にお世話になりました。この場を借りて御礼申し上げます。

2023年3月19日

冨野光太郎

Translator's Postface

It was in December, 2019, that I received Kazuo Kanai's first tanka collection, *Kaigai-ei* (TANKA from FOREIGN TRAVELS). As soon as I read it, I was struck by the breadth of his vision and the depth of his insight. I felt that this would undoubtedly evoke a great response and excitement not only among Japanese poets, but poets overseas as well. Immediately, I selected three tanka from *Kaigai-ei*, translated them into English and French, and submitted them to *INTERNATIONAL TANKA* where they were published in issue 7, in May, 2020.

In the summer of 2021, Kazuo Kanai, who had read the tanka magazine, came to visit me and requested the translation of 112 tanka he had selected. I readily agreed because I believed that overseas readers would deepen their understanding of themselves through his tanka. Consequently, this collection of translated tanka, like a mirror, reflects foreign cultures seen through Japanese eyes to the rest of the world.

René Descartes said, "cogito, ergo sum" (I think, therefore I am). I think this is not wrong, but in order to understand oneself objectively, another step in the thinking process is needed, namely, verification through "cogitas, ergo sum" (you think, therefore I am). This collection fulfills that role for the readers.

Finally, I owe a lot to Yukiko Inoue Smith in the State of Washington, USA, for English, Fabrice Alessandro in Chiba, Japan, for French, and Maxianne Berger in Montreal, Canada, for the overall editing of English and French. I would like to express my sincere thanks to them.

March 19, 2023
Kotaro Tomino

Postface du Traducteur

C'était en décembre 2019 que j'ai reçu *Kaigai-ei* (TANKA de VOYAGES à l'ÉTRANGER), le premier recueil de tanka de Kazuo Kanai. Dès que je l'ai lu, j'ai été frappé par l'ampleur de sa vision et la profondeur de sa perspicacité. J'ai senti que cela susciterait sans aucun doute une grande réponse et un grand enthousiasme non seulement des poètes japonais, mais aussi des poètes à l'étranger. Immédiatement, j'ai sélectionné trois tanka de *Kaigai-ei*, je les ai traduits en anglais et en français, et je les ai soumis à *INTERNATIONAL TANKA* où ils parurent dans le numéro 7, publié en mai 2020.

À l'été 2021, Kazuo Kanai, qui avait lu la revue, est venu me rendre visite et m'a demandé la traduction de 112 tanka qu'il avait choisis. J'ai accepté sans hésiter parce que je croyais que les lecteurs à l'étranger approfondiraient leur compréhension d'eux-mêmes grâce à ses tanka. En conséquence, cette collection de tanka traduite, comme un miroir, reflète vers le reste du monde les cultures étrangères vues par des yeux japonais.

René Descartes a dit : « cogito, ergo sum » (Je pense, donc je suis). Je pense que ce n'est pas faux mais pour se comprendre objectivement, on doit avoir une étape supplémentaire du processus de réflexion, à savoir, la vérification de « cogitas, ergo sum » (Tu penses, donc je suis). Ce recueil remplit ce rôle pour les lecteurs.

Enfin, je dois beaucoup à Yukiko Inoue Smith dans l'état de Washington aux États-Unis pour l'anglais, à Fabrice Alessandro à Chiba au Japon pour le français et à Maxianne Berger à Montréal au Canada pour la révision générale de l'anglais et du français. Je tiens à leur exprimer mes remerciements sincères.

le 19 mars 2023
Kotaro Tomino

プロフィール

金井一夫　著者
1936年　東京、向島生まれ、現在、千葉県八千代市在住
1952年　全国珠算検定試験1級合格
1962年　中央大学商学部卒
1966年　公認会計士資格取得
1967年　税理士資格取得
1975-95年　日本公認会計士協会理事、常務理事、副会長を歴任
1983年　千葉県八千代市市議会議員
1998年　藍綬褒章受章
2009年　旭日小綬章受賞
2011年　ライオンズクラブ国際協会333C地区ガバナー就任
2018年　同トップ・テン・ユースキャンプ及び交換委員長賞受賞
－歌歴－
2000年　短歌『ひこばえ』入会
2001年　『塔』短歌会入会、東京歌会に所属
2004年　『歩道』短歌会入会、『マルタの会』入会
　　　　日本歌人クラブ会員、千葉県歌人クラブ会員
2020年　国際タンカ協会会員

冨野光太郎　訳者
1948年　名古屋生まれ
1972年　東京外国語大学仏語学科卒
1985年　米国ロチェスター大学MBA
2013年　住友金属鉱山(株)顧問退任
2015年　日本歌人クラブ会員
2016年　千葉県歌人クラブ会員
2017年　国際タンカ協会会員

Maxianne Berger　監修者
1949年　カナダ・トロント生まれ、モントリオール育ち
1973年　マギル大学聴覚学修士
1996年　コンコルディア大学文学修士
2005年　『短歌カナダ』会員
2010年　カナダ文学翻訳者協会会員
2012-17年　日本歌人クラブ『タンカ・ジャーナル』会員
2014-19年　カナダ短歌誌 Cirrus を Mike Montreuil と共同編集
2017年　国際タンカ協会会員

PROFILES

Kazuo Kanai: Author

1936 Born in Mukōjima, Tokyo, and lives in Yachiyo-city, Chiba
1952 The top level of the National Examination of Abacus
1962 B.A. Chūō University, Commercial Science
1966 Certified public accountant
1967 Certified tax accountant
1975 Served as director, managing director, and vice president
 -95 of the Japanese Institute of Certified Public Accountants
1983 Yachiyo City Councilor, Chiba Prefecture, Japan
1998 Decorated with the Blue Ribbon Medal of Honour
2009 Decorated with the Order of the Rising Sun, Gold Rays and Rosette
2011 District governor of Lions Clubs International Association 333C
2018 Top Ten Youth Camps and Exchange Chair Award of Lions Club
-Tanka Activities-
2000 Tanka Group "HIKOBAE"
2001 Member of "TŌ" Tanka Society, Tokyo Branch
2004 Member of "HODŌ" Tanka Society and the Society of Tanka "Martha"
 Member of The Japan Tanka Poets' Society
 Member of Chiba Prefecture Tanka Poets' Club
2020 Member of International Tanka Society

Kotaro Tomino: Translator

1948 Born in Nagoya, Japan
1972 B.A. Tokyo University of Foreign Studies, French dept.
1985 MBA University of Rochester, USA
2013 Retired from Sumitomo Metal Mining Co., Ltd.
2015 Member of The Japan Tanka Poets' Society
2016 Member of Chiba Prefecture Tanka Poets' Club
2017 Member of International Tanka Society

Maxianne Berger: Editing & Research

1949 Born in Toronto. Family returns Montreal.
1973 M. Sc. (Appl), Audiology, McGill University, Montreal
1996 M.A. English Literature, Concordia University, Montreal
2005 Member of Tanka Canada
2010 Member of the Association of Literary Translators of Canada
2012-17 Member of Tanka Journal, The Japan Tanka Poets' Society
2014-19 Co-editor (with Mike Montreuil) of *Cirrus: tankas de nos jours*
2017 Member of International Tanka Society

PROFILS

Kazuo Kanai, l'Auteur

1936 Né à Mukōjima, Tokyo, et vit à Yachiyo, Chiba
1952 Niveau supérieur de l'examen national de boulier
1962 Université Chūō, Sciences commerciales
1966 Diplôme d'expert-comptable
1967 Diplôme de consultant fiscal
1975 Directeur, directeur général et vice-président
-95 de l'Institut japonais des experts-comptables agréés
1983 Conseiller municipal à Yachiyo, Préfecture de Chiba, Japon
1998 Décoré de la Médaille au ruban bleu
2009 Décoré de l'Ordre du Soleil Levant, Rayons d'Or et Rosette
2011 Gouverneur de district de l'Association internationale du Lions Club 333C
2018 Prix du « Top Ten Youth Camps and Exchange Chair » du Lions Club
-Activités de Tanka-
2000 Membre du Groupe de Tanka « HIKOBAE »
2001 Membre de la Société deTanka « TŌ », à la branche de Tokyo
2004 Membre de la Société deTanka « HODŌ » et « Martha »
　　　Membre du Club des poètes de tanka japonais
　　　Membre du Club des poètes de tanka de la préfecture de Chiba
2020 Membre de l'International Tanka Society

Kotaro Tomino: Traducteur

1948 Né à Nagoya, Japon
1972 Université des études étrangères de Tokyo, dépt. de français
1985 MBA Université de Rochester, les États-Unis
2013 Retraité de Sumitomo Metal Mining Co., Ltd.
2015 Membre du Club des Poètes de tanka japonais
2016 Membre du Club des poètes de tanka de la préfecture de Chiba
2017 Membre de l'International Tanka Society

Maxianne Berger: Révision et Recherche

1949 Née à Toronto. La famille retourne à Montréal.
1973 M.Sc. (Appl.) Audiologie, Université McGill, Montréal
1996 M.A. Littérature anglaise, Université Concordia, Montréal
2005 Membre de Tanka Canada
2010 Membre de l'Association des traductrices et traducteurs littéraires du Canada
2012-17 Membre du Tanka Journal, Club des poètes de tanka japonais
2014-19 Co-directrice (avec Mike Montreuil) de la revue *Cirrus:tankas de nos jours*
2017 Membre de l'International Tanka Society

●E-mail Address

金井一夫
Kazuo Kanai ·············· kazkanai@tempo.ocn.ne.jp
冨野光太郎
Kotaro Tomino ········ oratok6132@ozzio.jp

TANKA from FOREIGN TRAVELS
112 Tanka by Kazuo Kanai
in three languages

TANKA de VOYAGES à l'ÉTRANGER
112 tanka par Kazuo Kanai
en trois langues

Author / l'Auteur : Kazuo Kanai
Translator / Traducteur : Kotaro Tomino
Editing and Research / Révision et Recherche : Maxianne Berger
Book designer / Maquettiste : Shota Takabayashi

英仏訳

海外詠112首

2023年7月7日　発行

著　者　金井一夫
訳　者　冨野光太郎
監　修　マクシアンヌ・バーガー
発行者　齋藤愼爾
発行所　深夜叢書社
　　　　〒176-0006
　　　　東京都練馬区栄町2-10-403
　　　　info@shinyasosho.com

装丁　髙林昭太
印刷・製本　株式会社東京印書館